HOT DOG

Doug Salati

Alfred A. Knopf   New York

For Mia & Sami

THIS IS A BORZOI BOOK PUBLISHED BY ALFRED A. KNOPF

Copyright © 2022 by Doug Salati

All rights reserved. Published in the United States by
Alfred A. Knopf, an imprint of Random House Children's
Books, a division of Penguin Random House LLC,
New York. Knopf, Borzoi Books, and the colophon are
registered trademarks of Penguin Random House LLC.

Visit us on the Web! rhcbooks.com
Educators and librarians, for a variety of teaching tools,
visit us at RHTeachersLibrarians.com
Library of Congress Cataloging-in-Publication Data
is available upon request.
ISBN 978-0-593-30843-1 (trade)
ISBN 978-0-593-30844-8 (lib. bdg.)
ISBN 978-0-593-30845-5 (ebook)

The text of this book is set in 18-point Bell MT Pro.

The illustrations were created using a combination
of pencil and gouache on paper and Photoshop.

Book design by Rachael Cole

MANUFACTURED IN THE UNITED STATES OF AMERICA
April 2022
10 9 8 7 6 5 4
First Edition

C ity

summer

steamy

sidewalks

concrete

crumbles

sirens

screech

so hot!

can't sit

or sniff

or wait

crowds

close in . . .

too close!

too loud!

too much!

THAT'S IT!

won't move
one bit

a slow escape

unfolding sky, a salty breeze

a welcome whiff of someplace new

an island . . . wild and long and low

here, a pup can *run*

sun sinks down, swallowed by the sea

moon rises, skyline shimmers

trains
rumble and hum

familiar scents

a rush of wind

everyone

cools

down

happy for home
hungry for supper

what a day for a dog!

ready to leap

into a deep

ocean

sleep